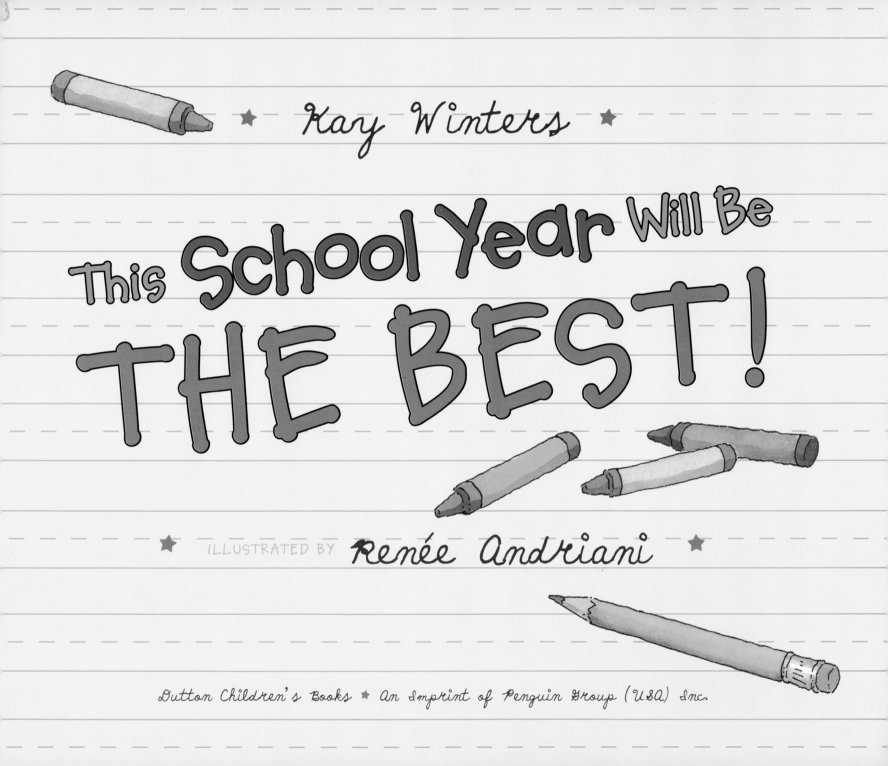

★ Kay Winters ★

This School Year Will Be THE BEST!

★ ILLUSTRATED BY Renée Andriani ★

Dutton Children's Books ★ An Imprint of Penguin Group (USA) Inc.

To Linda Dicker, teacher, and Eileen Wessel, principal,
who know how to make each school year be the BEST!
—K.W.

To the terrific teachers and students
at Corinth Elementary School in Prairie Village, Kansas
—R.A.

DUTTON CHILDREN'S BOOKS
A division of Penguin Young Readers Group
Published by the Penguin Group
Penguin Group (USA) Inc., 375 Hudson Street, New York, New York 10014, U.S.A.
Penguin Group (Canada), 90 Eglinton Avenue East, Suite 700, Toronto, Ontario M4P 2Y3, Canada
    (a division of Pearson Penguin Canada Inc.)
Penguin Books Ltd, 80 Strand, London WC2R 0RL, England
Penguin Ireland, 25 St Stephen's Green, Dublin 2, Ireland (a division of Penguin Books Ltd)
Penguin Group (Australia), 250 Camberwell Road, Camberwell, Victoria 3124, Australia
    (a division of Pearson Australia Group Pty Ltd)
Penguin Books India Pvt Ltd, 11 Community Centre, Panchsheel Park, New Delhi - 110 017, India
Penguin Group (NZ), 67 Apollo Drive, Rosedale, North Shore 0632, New Zealand (a division of Pearson New Zealand Ltd)
Penguin Books (South Africa) (Pty) Ltd, 24 Sturdee Avenue, Rosebank, Johannesburg 2196, South Africa
Penguin Books Ltd, Registered Offices: 80 Strand, London WC2R 0RL, England

CIP Data is available.

Published in the United States by Dutton Children's Books,
a division of Penguin Young Readers Group
345 Hudson Street, New York, New York 10014
www.penguin.com/youngreaders

Designed by IRENE VANDERVOORT

Manufactured in China   First Edition

ISBN 978-0-525-42275-4

10 9

Today was the first day of school.

We went to the rug and sat in a circle.
Our teacher asked, "What do you hope will
happen this year?"

We each shared a wish. I went first.

I hope I get the *best seat* on the bus.

This year I hope
I'll remember
my **homework**.

I'll look good
in my school picture.

We'll have a **chocolate fountain** at lunch!

This year
I'll kick the ball into
the right goal.

On the day the fire truck comes,
I'll be the one to **squirt the hose**.

We'll take **a field trip**
to someplace really cool.

I hope **I won't be a vegetable** in our school play!

I want to take the class pet home for winter break.

Our mom will bring a
BIRTHDAY SURPRISE to school.

I hope we get at least **one snow day**.

This year I'll **win the science fair.**

I hope I'll *make friends* in my new school.

When the nurse measures me,
I'll be tall.

I hope our *butterflies* will hatch.

We'll have **SKATEBOARD DAY**.

I won't **Lose things** in my desk.

The principal will
dO SOMeTHING CRazy!

My *report card*
will be perfect!

Then our teacher told us her wish.

I'll **get to know** each one of you.